STORY NUMBER 2

STORY NUM

A Harlin Quist Book

Published by Harlin Quist, Incorporated.
Library of Congress Catalog Card: 78-70568.

BER 2

BY EUGENE IONESCO
WITH PICTURES
BY GERARD FAILLY

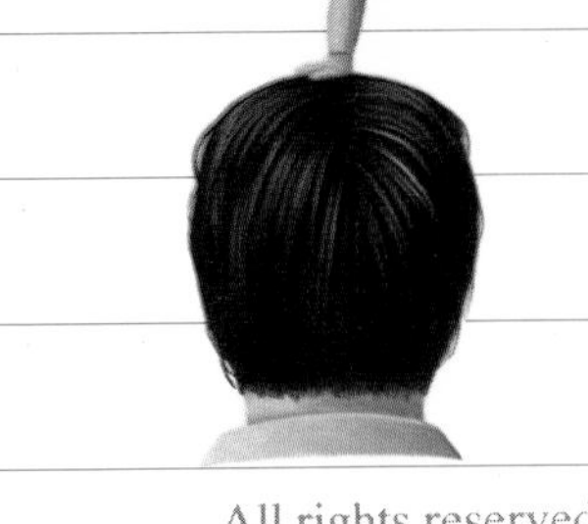

ISBN: 0-8252-8282-9 for the paperback,

0-8252-8172-5 for the hardcover.
Translated by Calvin K. Towle.

Designed by Patrick Couratin.
First printing. Printed in the U.S.A.

One morning, Josette's papa got up early. He had slept well because he had not gone to a restaurant the night before to eat sauerkraut. He had not gone to the theatre either, or to a nightclub, or to a puppet show. He had not gone to the fair to eat onion soup. He had not even eaten sauerkraut at home. The doctor had warned him not to. Papa is on a diet. He

was very hungry last night, so he went to bed very early – because, as the saying goes, a good sleep is a meal in itself.

Josette knocked on the door of her parents' room. Mama had left. Mama was not in bed. Maybe she was under the bed. Maybe she was in the closet. But the closet was locked. Josette could not see her mama anywhere.

Jacqueline, the maid, told Josette that her mama had left early because she too had

gone to bed very early. She had not been to a restaurant. She had not been to a puppet show. She had not been to the theatre. She had not eaten sauerkraut.

Jacqueline told Josette that her mama had just left the house, with her pink umbrella, her pink gloves, her pink shoes, her pink hat with flowers on the hat, her pink pocketbook with the little mirror in it, her pretty flowered dress, her lovely flowered coat, her beautiful flowered stockings, with a gorgeous bouquet of flowers

in her hand. Mama is very stylish. Mama has beautiful eyes, like two flowers. She has a mouth like a flower. She has a little pink nose, like a flower. She has hair like flowers. She has flowers in her hair.

Now Josette goes to see her papa at his office. Papa is on the telephone. He smokes, and he speaks into the telephone. He says: "Hello, sir, hello. Is that you? I told you never to call me again. Sir, you bore me. Sir, I haven't a second to lose."

Josette says to her papa, "Are you talking on the telephone?"

Papa hangs up. He says, "This is not a telephone."

"Yes, it is," Josette answers. "Mama told me so. Jacqueline said so too."

"Your mama and Jacqueline are wrong," papa says. "Your mama and Jacqueline don't know what it's called. It's called a cheese."

"That's called a cheese?" asks Josette. "Then people are going to think it's made of cheese."

"No," says papa, "because cheese isn't called cheese. It's called music box. And the music box is called a rug. The rug is called a lamp. The ceiling is called floor. The floor is called ceiling. The wall is called a door."

So papa teaches Josette the real meaning of

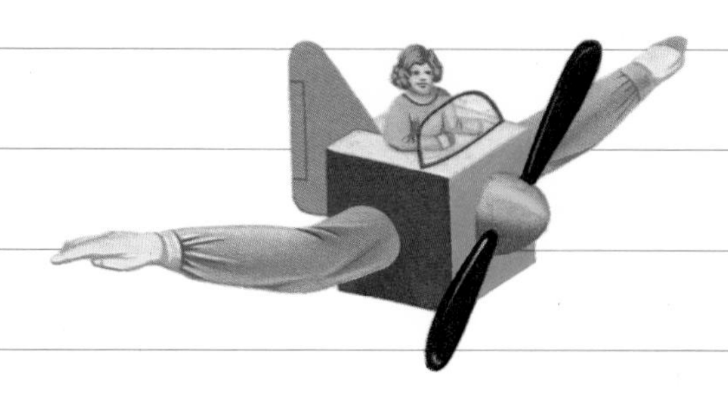

words. A chair is a window. The window is a penholder. A pillow is a piece of bread. Bread is a bedside rug. Feet are ears. Arms are feet. A head is a behind. A behind is a head. Eyes are fingers. Fingers are eyes.

Then Josette speaks the way her father teaches her. She says : “I look out the chair while eating my pillow. I walk with my ears. I have ten eyes to walk with and two fingers to look with. I sit down with my head on the floor. I put my behind on the ceiling. When I have eaten the music box, I put jam on the bedside

rug, for a good dessert. Take the window, papa, and draw me some pictures.”

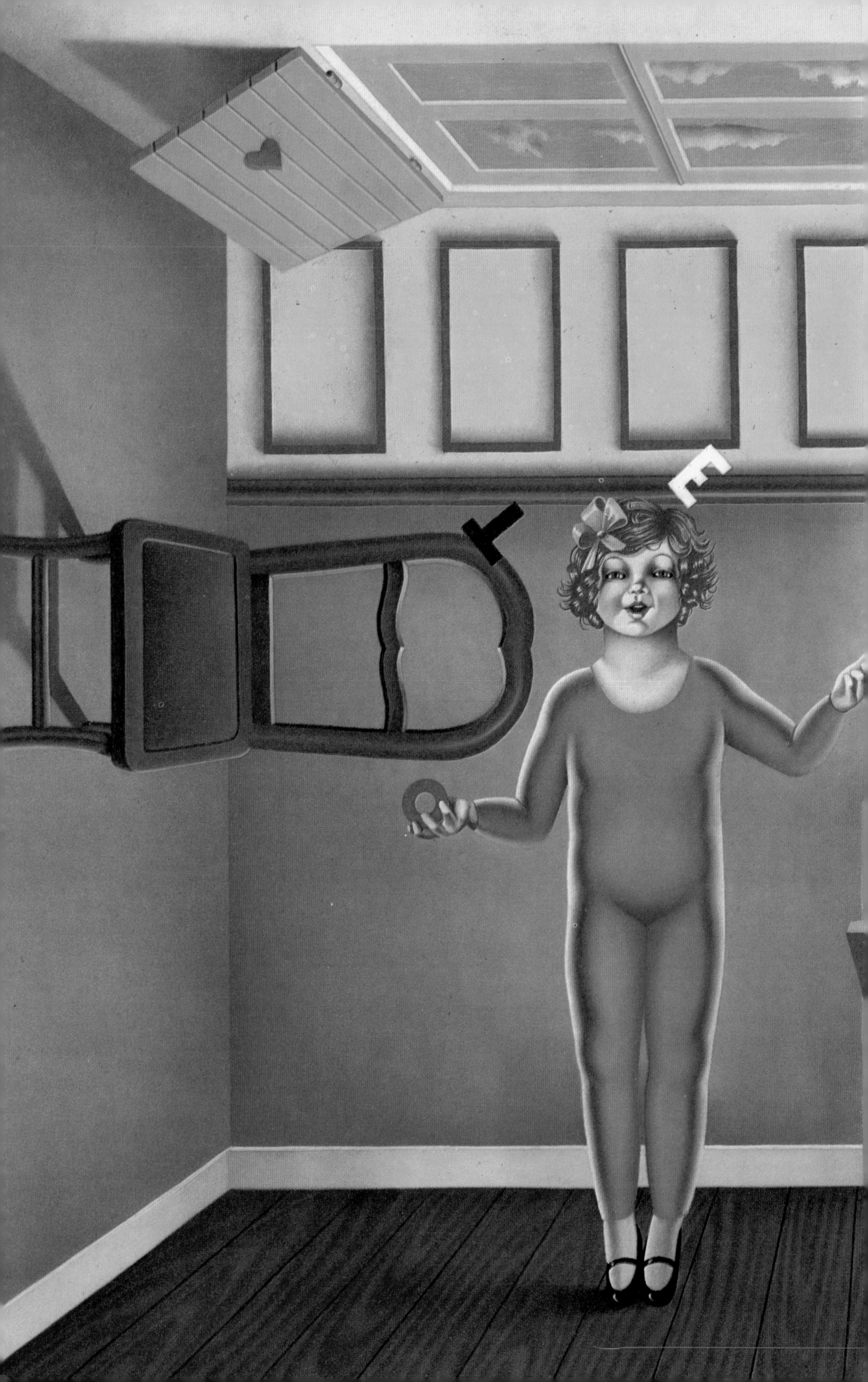

Josette is doubtful about one thing. “What are pictures called?” she asks.

“Pictures?” says papa. “What are pictures called? One musn’t say *pictures!* One must say *pictures.*”

At this moment Jacqueline comes in. Josette races toward her and says to her : “You know,

Jacqueline, pictures aren’t pictures. Pictures are pictures.”

“Ah,” Jacqueline says, “more of her father’s foolishness. But of course, my dear, pictures aren’t called pictures. They’re called pictures.”

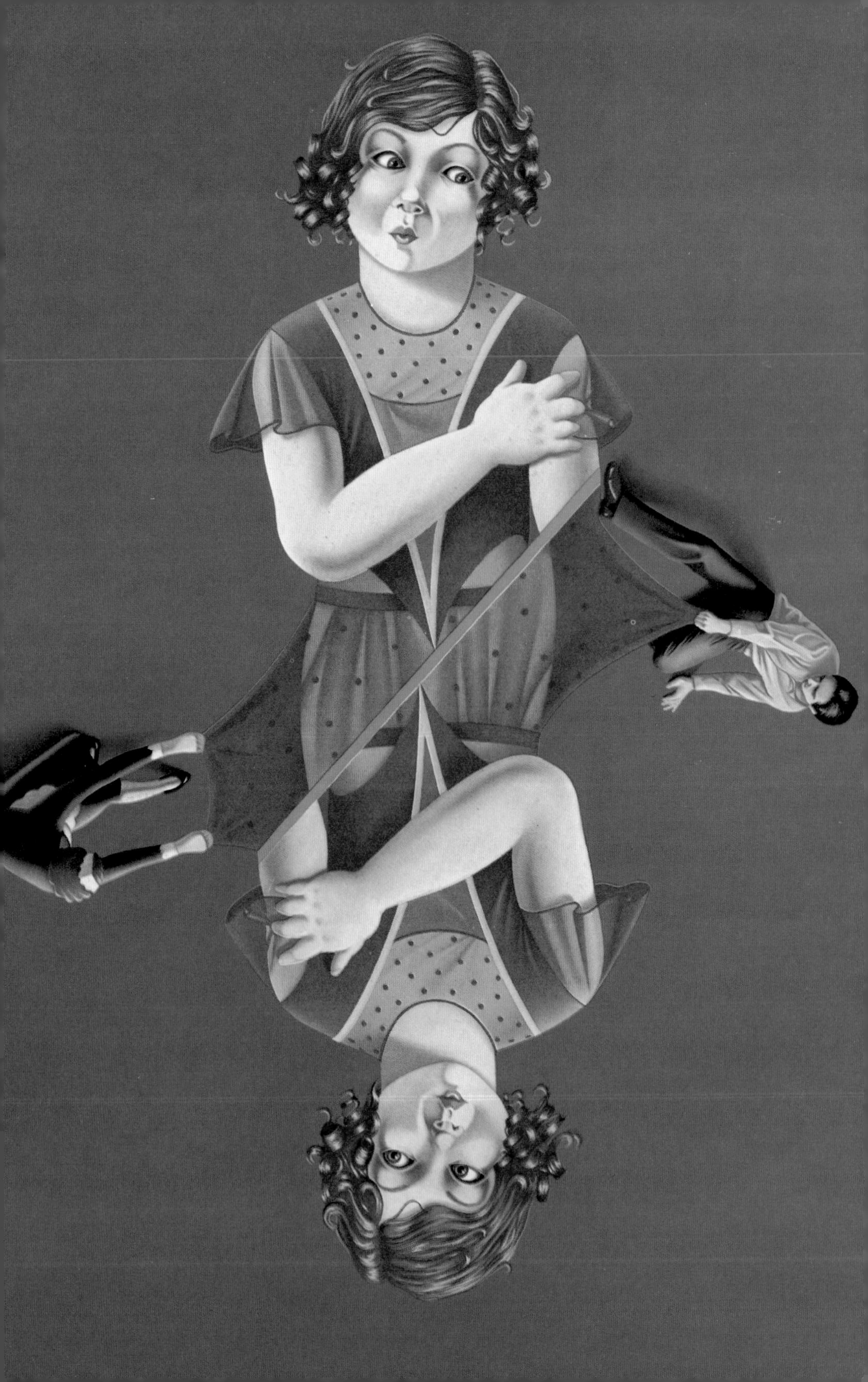

Then papa tells Jacqueline, "What Josette says to you is right."

"No," Jacqueline replies. "She says the opposite."

"No," says papa to Jacqueline. "You're the one who says the opposite."

"No. It's you."

"No. It's you."

"You're both saying the same thing," Josette tells them.

Suddenly mama arrives, like a flower, in her flowered dress, carrying flowers, with her flowered pocketbook, her flowered hat, her eyes like flowers, her mouth like a flower.

"What have you been doing out so early?" papa asks.

"Gathering flowers," says mama.

And Josette says, "Mama, you opened the wall."